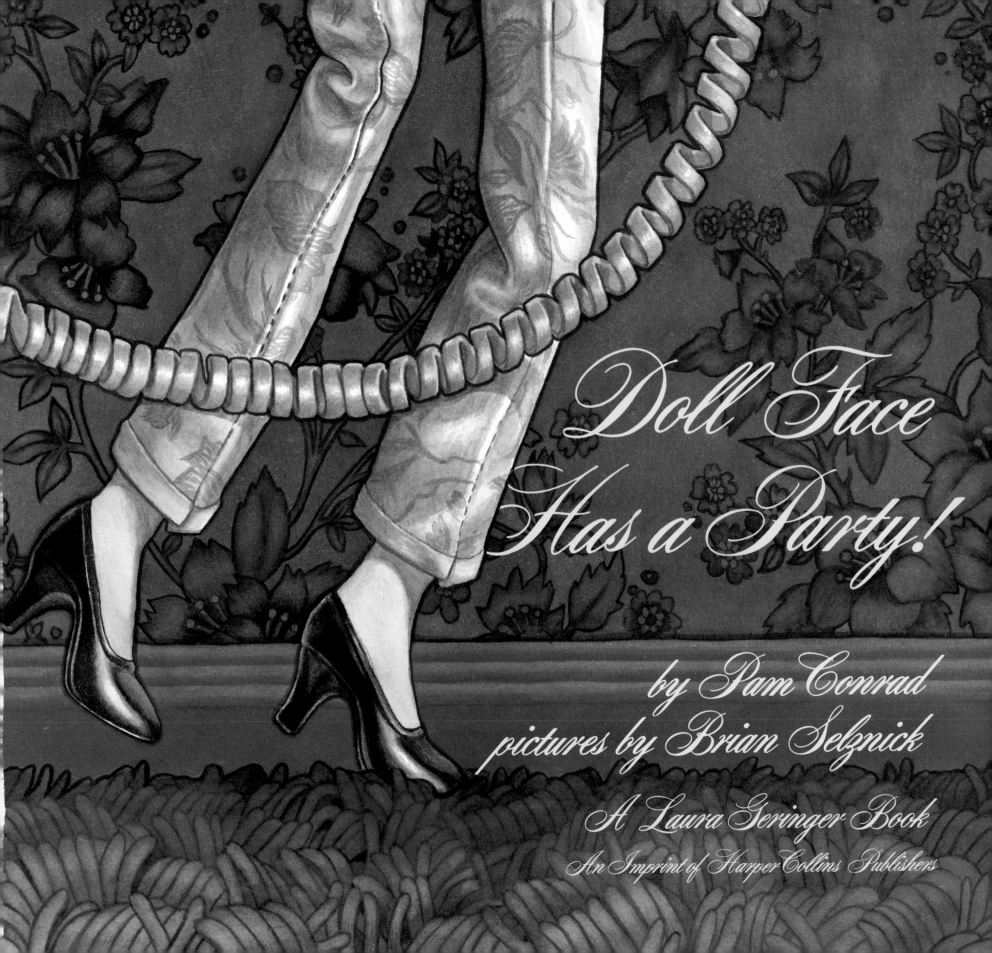

Doll Face
Has a Party!

by Pam Conrad

pictures by Brian Selznick

A Laura Geringer Book
An Imprint of HarperCollins Publishers

*D*oll Face loved a party.

So one morning she called up all her friends. "There will be a party today with music and dancing and Sweet Cake. Please come at noon."

Everyone was excited, because they all liked music and dancing and Sweet Cake. And they all loved Doll Face.

So Doll Face put a table in the sun. She covered it with a bright-blue tablecloth and set it with her favorite Plate.

To the Plate she said, "You must be very still."

She added a Fork on one side of the Plate.

"And you must be very straight."

Then the Cup. "Cup, stay empty until I fill you with tea."

Doll Face put a Spoon on the other side of the plate.

"Later you will stir the tea.

"And Knife," she said, "you will cut Sweet Cake."

Then Doll Face put out a Teapot full of mint tea in the center of the table.

"Teapot, wait right here and keep the tea hot while I find some music and Sweet Cake."

Then Doll Face went off looking.

She met a Chair in the middle of a rug. "I need music for my party," she said. "Can you make music?"

"I can't make music, Doll Face, but I am excellent at parties. You can sit on me when you're not dancing."

"Then you are invited to my party, Chair. Follow me and we'll find music and Sweet Cake."

"I'm no good at finding things either, but I know someone who is," said Chair. He stirred the slightest bit, and a shiny yellow Balloon rose up from behind him.

"Did I hear 'party'?" cried the Balloon. "I love a party! How can I help?"

Doll Face clapped her hands and laughed. "All we need now is music and Sweet Cake."

Doll Face, Chair, and Balloon went off looking for music and Sweet Cake.

Balloon led the way. He floated in the air before Doll Face and held her hand. Chair followed.

"We've come so far, Balloon, and still no music. Still no Sweet Cake, and I'm tired," said Doll Face.

"Have a seat," said Chair. And Doll Face and Balloon sat down together to think.

Balloon frowned and tangled his string. "I know I heard music here somewhere," he said. "Just yesterday."

"Dink, dink," said someone on a shelf. "What's this?"

"Oh," said Doll Face sadly, "we're looking for music and Sweet Cake. And we can't find them anywhere."

"Dink a diddle dink a clink," said the voice on the shelf. "Will I do?"

Doll Face stood on Chair to see high on the shelf, and there was a Little Red Piano. Dink a dink.

"You are just what I'm looking for," said Doll Face. "Can you make dancing music?"

The Piano answered with a waltz. "Ba-dink, clink, clink. Ba-dink, clink, clink."

Very carefully, Doll Face slid Little Red Piano off the shelf and tucked it under her arm. "Now we have music for my party."

"Let's go to the party," said Balloon, jumping along the back of Chair.

"Not so fast, Balloon," said Chair. "There's one other thing."

Doll Face was sad. She sat down in the Chair and put the Piano on her lap. "Where will we ever find Sweet Cake?" she asked. Balloon tapped against her shoulder and listened while Doll Face tapped out a sad tune.

"Da-doon, diddle, doon, ba-doon."

"Goodness, Piano," said Doll Face. "Your keys are sticky."

"Yes," said Piano. "Someone was playing a jig on me yesterday while they were eating Sweet Cake."

"Sweet Cake! Sweet Cake? And where was this Sweet Cake?" asked Chair.

"Well, if you play a little march, I will lead you there," said Piano.

So Doll Face tapped a lively march on the Piano, and off they went. They marched through the long hall with the echo and the pictures on the walls.

"Was the Sweet Cake here?"
whispered Balloon.
"Not here," said Piano.

They marched into the dining room, with its long table and heavy wooden chairs.

"Is this the place?" asked Chair.

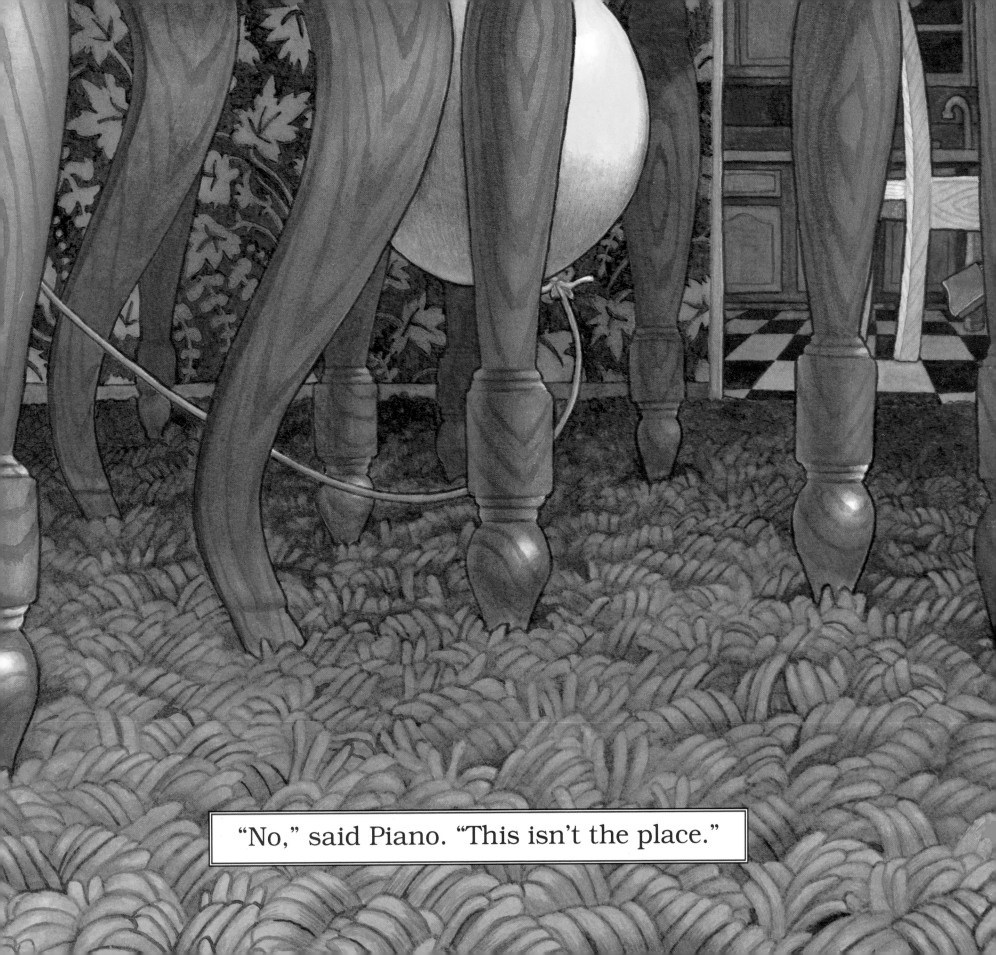

"No," said Piano. "This isn't the place."

Then they came to the kitchen and marched across the black-and-white checkered floor. "This is the place," said Piano, and they all looked around them.

There was nothing on the table except a bowl of flowers.

There was nothing on the stove except a pot of simmering soup.

But there on the counter, sitting on a paper-lace doily, was the most beautiful cake with pink-and-white icing and tiny green sugar leaves.

"Look," whispered Chair to Doll Face. "Look! Sweet Cake!"

"Now we can have our party!" said Balloon. "We have everything we need!"

Doll Face, Chair, Balloon, Little Red Piano, and the Sweet Cake came marching back. Piano played the marching tune. "Dink a dink, clink a clink. Dink a dink, plip plip."

"She's back!" Fork shouted. "Doll Face is back! Can we start the party? Are we ready?"

"We heard the music," Knife said. "We heard the music before we saw you!"

"Yes, we have music for the party," said Spoon.

"And there's a Balloon, too," shouted Plate.

"And a comfortable Chair for resting between dances," said Cup.

Teapot felt all warm inside. "Let the party begin," she said.

And so it did.

Doll Face cut the Sweet Cake with Knife and gave herself the biggest piece, right in the center of Plate.

She sat on Chair and ate the Sweet Cake with Fork while she tapped her toe and watched everyone dancing to the music.

Then she poured herself a cup of tea from steaming Teapot, stirred it with Spoon, and sipped it slowly.

Doll Face danced with Balloon, and she danced with Teapot. She danced with everybody, and between dances they all sat on Chair.

It was a wonderful party.

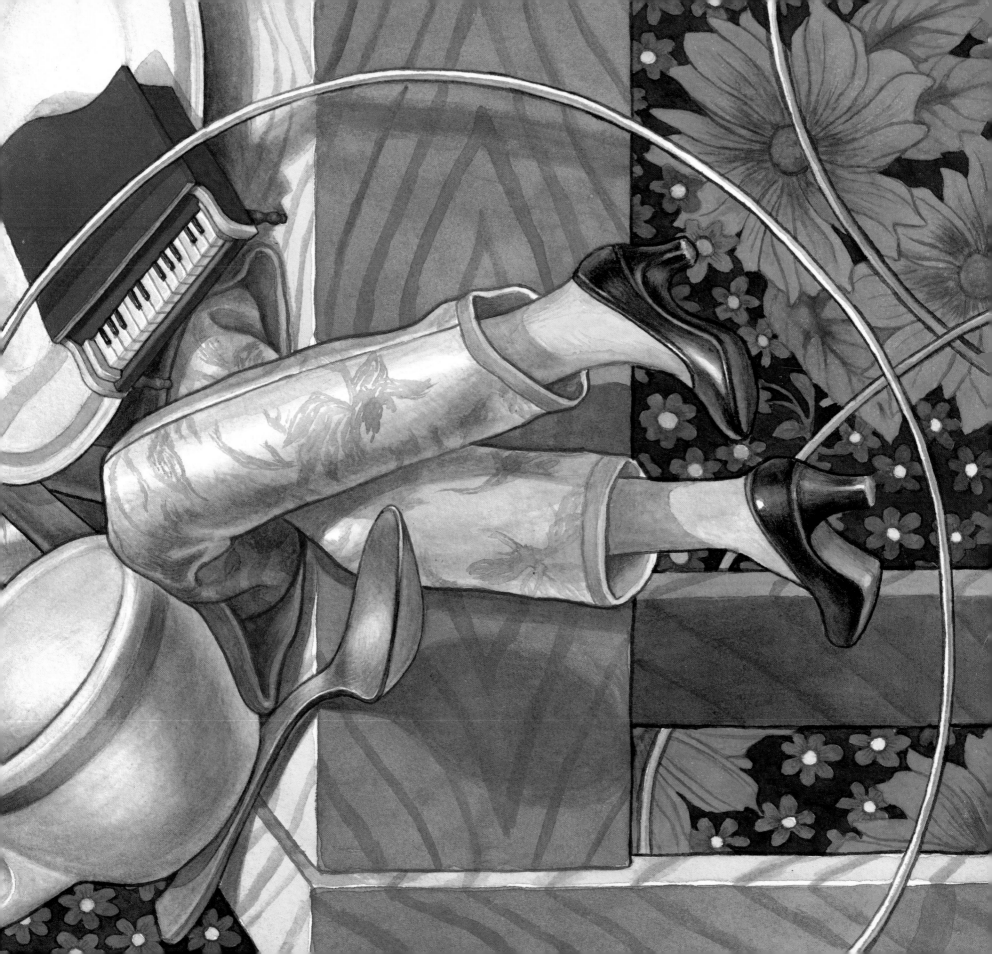

For Bill Morris,
who really knows how to throw a party
—P.C.


For Laura Geringer
—B.S.

*Doll Face Has a Party!*
*Text copyright © 1994 by Pam Conrad*
*Illustrations copyright © 1994 by Brian Selznick*
*Printed in the U.S.A. All rights reserved.*

*Library of Congress Cataloging-in-Publication Data*
*Conrad, Pam.*
  *Doll Face has a party! / Pam Conrad ; illustrations by Brian Selznick.*
    *p.      cm.*
  *"A Laura Geringer book."*
  *Summary: When Doll Face can't find Sweet Cake for her party, a chair,*
*a tiny tin piano, and a whispering balloon come to life to help her find the*
*finishing touch to her soirée.*
  *ISBN 0-06-024262-0. — ISBN 0-06-024263-9 (lib. bdg.)*
  *[1. Dolls—Fiction.   2. Parties—Fiction.]   I. Selznick, Brian,  ill.*
*II. Title.*
*PZ7.C76476Do   1994                                                    93-33207*
*[E]—dc20                                                                    CIP*
                                                                              *AC*

*Typography by Tom Starace*
*1   2   3   4   5   6   7   8   9   10*
❖
*First Edition*